D1094186

WE CAN READ!™

Aloha!

by Jacqueline Sweeney

photography by G. K. & Vikki Hart
photo illustration by Blind Mice Studio

BENCHMARK BOOKS

MARSHALL CAVENDISH
NEW YORK

Aloha! to Dash and Theo,
Kelly Lucille Schweizer, and
Liam Robert Day—welcome, little ones.

With thanks to Daria Murphy, principal of Scotchtown
Elementary School, Goshen, New York
and former reading specialist, for reading this
manuscript with care and for writing the
"We Can Read and Learn" activity guide.

Benchmark Books
Marshall Cavendish
99 White Plains Road
Tarrytown, New York 10591
www.marshallcavendish.com

Text copyright © 2003 by Jacqueline Sweeney
Photo illustrations © 2003 by G.K. & Vikki Hart
and Mark and Kendra Empey

Library of Congress Cataloging-in-Publication Data
Sweeney, Jacqueline.
Aloha! /by Jacqueline Sweeney.
p.   cm. — (We can read!)
Summary: Four animal friends travel to Hawaii, where they are shown
the sights, told a story, and taught a song by their gecko guide.
ISBN 0-7614-1510-6
[1. Hawaii—Fiction. 2. Travel—Fiction. 3. Animals—Fiction.] I. Title.
PZ7.S974255 Al 2002   [E]—dc21   2002003235

Printed in Italy

1 3 5 6 4 2

Characters

Hildy

Gus

Molly

Ladybug

Kono

F*lap*

Flap

THUNK!

"Ow! My head," quacked Hildy.

"Where are we?"

"Locked in a box," said Gus.

"Something's out there!" squeaked Molly.

"Push," chirped a voice. "Push up!"

"UMPH!" huffed the friends.

Up popped the lid!

Out plopped

Hildy, Molly, Ladybug, and Gus.

Chick-chak

Chick-chak

"Aloha!" said a lizard.

"Welcome to Hawaii."

Fron

"Who are you?" asked Molly.

"*What* are you?" asked Ladybug.

"My name is Kono," said the lizard.

"I'm a gecko."

He leaped to a window.

"And I have sticky feet."

"How did we get here?" asked Gus.

"You came in a box."

From: Sara Salamander
Willow Pond

To: Kono Gecko
Hawaii

"I need to *fly*," fluttered Ladybug.

"I need to *swim*," quacked Hildy.

"I need to *eat*," said Gus.

Kono leaped on Gus's back.

"Wiki-wiki," he chirped.

"Hurry up!"

WHOOSH-SH-SH

WHOOSH-SH-SH

"What's that sound?"
Molly shouted.
"That's kai," yelled Kono,
"the sea."

WHOMP!

WHOMP!

"What was that?" cried Hildy.

"Coconuts!" yelled Kono.

One coconut cracked open.

The friends sat down to eat.

19

While they ate,

Kono told a story of Moo.

"A giant lizard," he said,

"Moo comes at night.

He comes in silver light!"

"Moo is scary,"

shivered Gus.

20

Kono talked everyone to sleep.
When they woke it was night.
"Look!" cried Ladybug.
"Silver water, silver trees!"
"It's Moo!" screamed Gus.
"He comes in silver light!"

"Whoa!" chirped Kono.
"It's only the moon!"
He led his friends
down a sandy path.
"The moo—n will light
our way home."

"Teach us a song,"
quacked Hildy.

Kono sang:

Nani-lani—lovely sky
Lovely sea is nani-kai
Nani-mele—lovely song
Sing with me
You can't go wrong!

"*Nani-lani—lovely sky,*" sang Molly.

"*Lovely sea is nani-kai,*" sang Gus

"*Nani-mele—lovely song,*" sang Hildy.

"*Sing like geckos all night long,*"
chirped Kono.

And they did.

WE CAN READ AND LEARN

The following activities, which complement *Aloha!*, are designed to help children build skills in vocabulary, phonics, critical thinking, and creative writing.

CHALLENGE WORDS

The Hawaiian alphabet has only twelve letters—five vowels (a, e, i, o, u) and seven consonants (h, k, l, m, n, p, w). The vowels are pronounced as follows: **a**–*ah* as in "father"; **e**–*eh* as in "bet"; **i**–*ee* as in "see"; **o**–*oh* as in "sole"; **u**–*oo* as in "moon". Help children pronounce the Hawaiian words that appear in *Aloha!* Then discuss their meanings.

aloha	nani	Hawaii	wiki-wiki
mele	lani	kai	

Help children figure out the meanings of the following English words by focusing on the contexts in *Aloha!* in which they appear.

welcome	salamander	shivered	sticky
coconuts	gecko	giant	sandy
silver	huffed	friends	scary

GO HAWAIIAN!

Help children learn key facts about Hawaii including its state flower and flag. Children can draw the Hawaiian flag and then create a flag for the Willow Pond friends. They can also make a poster of Hawaiian highlights and decorate it with flowers, shells, and grass.

ISLAND GAMES AND FUN WITH PHONICS

The state of Hawaii is comprised of eight major islands and 124 minor islands. Do research on how the Hawaiian Islands were created. Help children locate the islands on a map and pinpoint the island (Hawaii, the Big Island) that the Willow Pond friends are on.

Cut out twelve island shapes from white paper and three wave shapes from blue paper. On each wave shape write one of the following endings: -s; -ed; -ing. Write the words listed below on the island shapes.

huff	quack	leap	crack
chirp	scream	shiver	squeak
ask	shout	yell	flutter

Tape one of the island shapes to a wall, and explain that islands are touched by waves on all sides. Tape the three wave shapes around the island shape. Explain that verbs are like islands and verb endings–like -s, -ed, and -ing–are like waves. Waves in general do not noticeably change the shape of an island, but they at least have a tiny effect on the shape of an island's edges, its shorelines. Verb endings do not completely change the sound and meaning of the verbs they "touch"; the change is slight. Say aloud the new word formed when each of the three waves touches the island taped to the wall. Then discuss the meanings of the new words. Repeat until the waves have touched all the islands. Have children use the words formed by the meeting of islands and waves in sentences. Record the sentences and write a new Hawaiian adventure for the Willow Pond friends.

THE GREAT GECKO AND HIS STICKY FEET

Ever hear of the Great Gecko? Children can learn about geckos and other lizards such as salamanders and newts by doing research at the library. Find out why geckos have sticky feet. What do they eat? How do they use their long tails? Children can choose one type of lizard, then research and draw it. Have children share their work to compare and contrast differences among lizards.

31

About the author

Jacqueline Sweeney is a poet and children's author. She has worked with children and teachers for over twenty-five years implementing writing workshops in schools throughout the United States. She specializes in motivating reluctant writers and shares her creative teaching methods in numerous professional books for teachers. Her most recent work includes the Benchmark Books series *Kids Express*, a series of anthologies of poetry and art by children, which she conceived of and edited. She lives in Catskill, New York.

About the photo illustrations

The photo illustrations are the collaborative effort of photographers G. K. and Vikki Hart and Mark and Kendra Empey of Blind Mice Studio. Following Mark Empey's sketched storyboard, G. K. and Vikki Hart photograph each animal and element individually. The images are then scanned and manipulated, pixel by pixel, by Mark and Kendra Empey at Blind Mice Studio. Each charming illustration may contain from 15 to 30 individual photographs.

All the animals that appear in this book were handled with love. They have been returned to or adopted by loving homes.

32